Little Witch's memorable Ha

Printed in the United Kingdom
ISBN: **978-1-80352-267-8**
Written and illustrated by David Bendall Sosa

E: cotopaxipublishing@post.com

This book is dedicated to Maisy, Charlie, Edie, Wilsy, Phoebe, Alice, Tom, Ed and Clara

LITTLE WITCH'S MEMORABLE HALLOWEEN

It was a cold, dry Halloween night.
And the silvery moon was so bright.
Sat upon a branch of the old oak tree,
were the outline of a group of three.
Little Witch, Spider Wise, and Goblin Dwight.
Their outline was created by the moon light.

Spider was wise, old, wrinkly, and hairy,
his body was as round as a blueberry.
With eight long prickly dark legs
and four eyes like a row of eggs.
And a smile that looked quite scary,
that made you feel rather wary.

Goblin Dwight was young and eager,
and always busy like a beaver.
He had a pair of extremely long pointed ears,
and a big nose capable of holding two beers.
He was sensitive and easily be reduced to tears.
Upsetting someone was one of his greatest fears.

Nestled upon Little Witch's head was a crooked hat.
She wore a long cloak, that looked like a large bat.
A scowl as if she had stood bare feet on a wet mat.
And sometimes she was known to be a little brat.
She seemed to be always ready for combat.
But occasionally she could be as nice as a pussy cat.

Spider Wise said to Little Witch "you seem to be blue."
"Wish I could turn back time and start a new."
Said Little Witch "and now I feel very sad,
I was angry and did something really bad."

"Oh, Dear what happened Little Witch?"
Asked Goblin Dwight with a nervous twitch.

"Two days ago, as I was walking home,
I was so hungry and angry; I kicked a gnome."
Goblin Dwight was absolutely horrified,
And was so upset he nearly cried.
Spider Wise was shocked and stunned,
that his round body became numbed.

"But that is not what made me sad,
That just made me feel really bad."
Said Little Witch looking quite mad.

"When I got home, I was mad with Broom.
No dinner and had not swept the room.
When I asked it, Why?
Broom told me it did try.
Not good enough, I shouted
and some abuse I spouted.
Threatened to throw Broom in the bin.
To which Broom gave me a cheeky grin.
I became so very mad,
that I did something so very bad.
I grabbed hold and shock Broom,
before I threw it around the room."

Spider Wise asked, "Was it upset?"
"It must have been, it left.
I was angry, crazy is what I had become,
And now I am feeling sad and glum.
Worst still I have lost my best chum."

"Your angry tantrums got you in trouble
And you may well end up in your own little bubble
You need to breath and count one, two, three.
Say anger has gone, now a nice person that's me"
Said Spider Wise to foolish Little Witch,
"You would be better suited to be happy rich"

Spider was such a wise old clever stick.
And could come up with a solution rather quick.
Goblin Dwight asked, "Is there any way we can help?"
Spider replied "Yes, tell her not to get angry and yelp."

Just then out of the silvery moonlit sky,
came a shadow that looked like a squashed pie.
"Is this a Halloween Party?" asked Batty Boin.
"Is it by invite or can anybody join?"

"Little Witch you look sorrowful and sour.
Spider you look as if you have lost all power.
And Goblin so melancholy in this Halloween hour."

Goblin whispered, "Tell him about Broom."
"In my anger I threw it around the room,
It has left for good I can only assume.
Now my little shack feels more like a tomb."
Little Witch meekly said, looking gloom.

"I wish I could tell Broom how sorry I am.
Come home, and have some bread and jam."
Said Little Witch with a tear in her eye,
which made poor Goblin Dwight cry.

"I see Broom fly over the forest every night.
Actually, I hear it, as I have poor sight.
Broom comes in from the west and heads east.
Must dash, wife has made me a Halloween feast."
Shouted Batty Boin, and off he flew.
Spider Wise exclaimed "I know what to do."

"Goblin Dwight your gardening skills are a pleasure to watch,
you grow such an abundance on your vegetable patch.
And early each morning out with watering can,
spraying fine mist of water across the garden span.
The water can spout is made of very fine holes.
I am sure they were made by the tiny claws of voles.
Goblin Dwight we need that watering can."
Said Spider Wise "As I have a special plan"

"Fill it with the purest spring water you can find,
and bring it back here if you be so kind.
Also bring back your dad's old spare bicycle wheel.
And rush back you don't have time to have a meal."

"Little Witch here are nine long strands of spider's web,
I want you to plait the strands into a rope" spider said
"Though the silk strands are as light as a feather,
when plaited they are far stronger than leather.
But we must continue to have dry weather."

It wasn't long before Little Witch got into a mess,
created a big knot and was getting in distress.
In a temper she threw the silk strands to the branch below.
When told to get them, in protest she moved slow.
"Be patient and don't get angry and shout,
when things do not seem to work out"

"When you are going to be angry and cross,
remember do not to let it be the boss.
You need to breath and count one, two, three.
Say anger has gone, now a nice person that's me"
Said Spider Wise in a calm and collected manner.
While thinking about creating a special banner.

"Be patient and slow when you plait at the start,
you will build up speed and be as fast as a go-cart."
Advised Spider Wise. My word he is so smart,
he deserves to be awarded a nice jam tart.

Little Witch took on board his advice, she started slow,
and built-up speed and soon there was a flow.
Half an hour later, she had completed her task.
"Spider Wise, what shall I do now" she would ask.

Spider was making a web attached to the branch below.
Busy weaving away, you could see the web grow.
A special web this seemed to be,
a little further down the oak tree.
It was not quite the usual type of cobweb seen.
It looked like something typed on a computer screen.

Goblin climbed up the tree with the spare wheel in hand,
and placed it in a small branch that looked like a stand.
With an old bicycle wheel, a pulley did he device
Little Witch remarked "This is such a surprise."

Goblin climbed back down the tree to the water can,
ready to tie both handle and spout as in the plan.
Spider took the rope, placed round the bicycle rim
And dropped half the rope down to him.

Little Witch pulled up the can of water, none spilt.
Spider Wise leaned on the can and put it on a tilt.
And a very fine spray of water was distilled,
down on to the cobweb Spider Wise had built.

It left lots of tiny droplets all along the special web,
as the droplets twinkled in the moonlight it read:

"SO SORRY BROOM,
PLEASE COME BACK
TO OUR LITTLE SHACK"

SO
SORRY
COME
TO
OUR
PLEASE
BACK
LITTLE
SHACK

And thirty minutes later guess who flew over?
Read the banner and felt the exposure.
Yes, it was Broom, it then came over,
hovered by Little Witch and smiled.
She promised that she would never be wild.

"Remember when you feel angry and cross
It is important not to let it be the boss.
You need to breath and count one, two, three.
Say anger has gone, now a nice person that's me."
said Spider Wise as he stood up in the oak tree.

She turned to Spider and Goblin and expressed her gratitude.
She said "The whole experience has changed my attitude"
Little Witch and Broom, flew off back to the shack
While Spider and Goblin made a Halloween snack
And maybe next Halloween, they will all come back.

Little Witch's memorable Halloween.